# A KNOCK AT THE DOOR

Story by Eric Sonderling
Illustration by Wendy Wassink Ackison

RSVP

RAINTREE
STECK-VAUGHN
PUBLISHERS
The Steck-Vaughn Company

Austin, Texas

To my grandma. I will always remember
all the stories she has told me. — E.S.

For my wonderful husband, Clark, who is my
best critic and most enthusiastic fan. — W.W.A.

**Publish-a-Book** is a trademark of Steck-Vaughn Company.

**Copyright © 1997 Steck-Vaughn Company.**

3 4 5 6 7 8 9 0   IP   01 00 99 98

For information on the Publish-a-Book™ Contest write to
Publish-a-Book™ Contest, P.O. Box 27010, Austin, TX 78755.

**Library of Congress Cataloging-in-Publication Data**

Sonderling, Eric, 1985 –
    A knock at the door / story by Eric Sonderling ; illustrations
by Wendy Wassink Ackison.
        p.    cm. — (Publish-a-book)
    Summary: Although they don't know anything about her, a
farmer and his wife take in a secretive, starving young woman
and allow her to hide on their isolated farm when the Nazis
come looking for her. Based on the experiences of the author's
grandmother.
    ISBN 0–8172–4434–4 (Hardcover)
    ISBN 0–8172–7211–9 (Softcover)
    1. World War, 1939–1945 — Germany — Juvenile fiction.
2. Jews — Germany — Juvenile fiction.   3. Children's writings,
American.  [1. World War, 1939–1945 — Germany — Fiction.
2. Jews — Germany — Fiction.   3. Children's writings.]
I. Ackison, Wendy Wassink, ill.   II. Title.   III. Series.
PZ7.S69747Kn   1997
[Fic]—dc21                              96-44841
                                                    CIP
                                                    AC

4

The year was 1944. It was a dark, cold, stormy night in Germany. There was a knock at the door. Mr. Schmidt opened the heavy wooden door. Standing there was a pale, cold, skinny teen-age girl.

Mr. Schmidt said, "You poor little girl. Please come in and warm yourself by the fire."

5

Mrs. Schmidt was shocked when she saw the girl. Her clothes were torn and ragged.

"Where have you come from?" exclaimed Mrs. Schmidt.

The girl did not answer. She just sat and stared at the fire. Mrs. Schmidt brought the girl a bowl of soup and some hot tea. The girl's eyes opened wide, and she took the food.

Mr. and Mrs. Schmidt couldn't believe how hungry the girl seemed to be. It was as if she had not eaten for days.

8

After she had eaten, the girl fell asleep on the floor by the fire. She did not wake up until the next day. The Schmidts felt very sorry for her, and they let her stay with them. They could not stop wondering who she was and where she had come from.

The Schmidts had a big farm. It was completely surrounded by the forest and was very isolated. The only way to get to the farm was by traveling through the forest. How had this girl found their house? Where had she come from? Where was her family?

After a few days, the girl finally spoke in a weak voice and said, "Thank you for letting me stay here. Please let me work for you, so that I can repay you."

Mrs. Schmidt asked, "What is your name? Where did you come from?" But the girl did not answer.

11

Mr. and Mrs. Schmidt needed help to take care of their big farm. They also felt sorry for the poor girl and did not want her to leave. They decided that they would wait to find out where she came from and who she was.

The girl was a very hard worker. She worked all day. She milked the cows and fed the chickens. The girl would even clean out the stable, although she was afraid of the big old brown horse.

She helped Mrs. Schmidt with the cooking and sewing. Mrs. Schmidt wondered about the girl. Someone had taught her how to sew and clean, but the girl never spoke about herself. This girl always seemed sad, and she never smiled.

As the months went by, the girl seemed to relax, and the Schmidts thought that she would tell them where she had come from. But she never did, and the Schmidts decided to wait until she was ready to tell them.

17

One day, there was a knock at the door. Mrs. Schmidt opened it. Standing in front of her was a horrible sight. It was a very tall, muscular man in a Nazi uniform. The man had a very mean face, and Mrs. Schmidt knew that there would be trouble. Mrs. Schmidt had not seen a Nazi for a long time, since her farm was so isolated.

"Is there a problem?" asked Mrs. Schmidt.

"If you have a Jew in your house, there is a problem!" snarled the Nazi.

"Why would I have a Jew in my house?" said Mrs. Schmidt.

"Well, there was an escape a few months ago. Four girls got away. We captured two and another was found dead. We think the fourth girl disappeared into the forest," explained the soldier.

Finally, Mrs. Schmidt realized who the girl was, and she said, "There is no Jew in my house. The girl must have died in the forest."

The Nazi pushed Mrs. Schmidt aside and said, "Well, I plan to look around here anyway."

Mrs. Schmidt was very scared. She did not want the poor girl to be captured by this Nazi. But there was nothing she could do about it.

23

The girl was cleaning out the stable when she saw the Nazi soldier. She knew she must hide, so she stayed in the barn and hid under the horse's hay. She was scared and shaking. The horse stood right over the pile of hay. When the soldier went into the barn, he noticed only the big old horse.

The Nazi finally left. The girl went back into the house where the Schmidts were standing by the fire. They looked very sad.

The girl said, "I will now tell you who I am and where I came from."

28

The girl told the Schmidts that her name was Berta and that she was eighteen years old. She was born in Poland, and her grandmother had a big farm. She had three brothers and a wonderful mother and father.

She said that when she was sixteen the Nazis took her from her family and put her in a concentration camp. She had been in the camp for two years when she finally escaped with three other girls. They all ran into the forest, but they were separated.

She did not know what had happened to the other girls. She was very frightened and thought about turning back, but she knew she would be killed if she went back to the camp. She lived in the forest for a few days until she reached the Schmidt's farm.

The Schmidts said, "Berta, you will stay with us until this terrible war is over."

Berta was never caught by the Nazis. After the war, she looked for her family. She finally found one brother in Sweden. None of the other family members had survived the war. Berta left Germany in 1947 and started a new life in the United States.

Eric Sonderling, author of **A Knock at the Door**, was born on February 4, 1985, in New York City. In May 1986, Eric and his family moved to Boca Raton, Florida. Eric attends Pine Crest School in Boca Raton. Eric has an older brother, Keith, who also attends Pine Crest School. Eric was elected vice president of the lower school at Pine Crest. He is a member of the Pine Crest Band and plays the baritone and clarinet. Eric loves cars and subscribes to many auto magazines.

In addition to winning the 1996 Publish-a-Book™ Contest, Eric was also chosen as the recipient of the 1996 Alexander Fischbein Young Writer's Award. This award was established in memory of Alex Fischbein, a writer who died at the age of ten, to encourage young students to write and submit their works for publication.

Eric's maternal grandparents are Holocaust survivors. His grandfather escaped the Warsaw ghetto and participated in the Nazi resistance movement. Eric was named in honor of his grandfather, who died three months before Eric was born. A very special relationship has developed between Eric and his grandmother, who was held in a concentration camp before she escaped. Eric seemed to sense that there was something very different about his grandmother. Eric's love for and genuine curiosity about his grandmother inspired her to speak about her experiences. Eric has spent many hours listening to his grandmother's stories. These stories include not only her sad experiences throughout the war, but also memories of her happy childhood in Poland before the war. *A Knock at the Door* is based on some of the stories that Eric's grandmother has told him. Eric hopes to write more books based on his grandmother's experiences.

The twenty honorable-mention winners in the **1996 Raintree/Steck-Vaughn Publish-a-Book™ Contest** were Amy Anderson, Joyce Kilmer School, Milltown, New Jersey; Meghan Codd, Riffenburgh Elementary School, Fort Collins, Colorado; Jonathan Cantwell, Ramblewood Elementary School, Coral Springs, Florida; Christopher Riedel, Haycock Elementary School, Falls Church, Virginia; Jonathan Jans, Jack Hille School, Oak Forest, Illinois; Kevin P. Barry, John Pettibone School, New Milford, Connecticut; Hiram Lew, St. Thomas Apostle School, San Francisco, California; Becky Kuplin, Sussex County Eastern District Library, Franklin, New Jersey; Amanda Marchetti, St. Joseph Memorial School, Hazleton, Pennsylvania; Julia K. Corley, Ruby Ray Swift Elementary School, Arlington, Texas; Sally Rees, Richards Elementary School, Whitefish Bay, Wisconsin; Katherine Connors, Haycock Elementary School, Falls Church, Virginia; Amanda R. Simpson, Mitchell Elementary School, Mitchell, Nebraska; Sarah Wexelbaum, Pine Crest School, Boca Raton, Florida; Matthew Ports, Hope Christian School, Albuquerque, New Mexico; Bridget Taylor, St. Anne's School, Bethlehem, Pennsylvania; Hillary Birtley, Clark Elementary School, St. Louis, Missouri; Chris Morin, Boulan Park Middle School, Troy, Michigan; Lauren Ferris, St. Vincent's Elementary School, Petaluma, California; Rula Assi, Juniper School, Escondido, California.

Wendy Wassink Ackison lives in Fayetteville, West Virginia, with her husband, Clark, and their two children, Nathan and Laurel. Wendy's father, Dr. W. K. Wassink, was a Dutch teen-ager growing up in Nazi-occupied Holland about the same time as this story about Eric's grandmother. When there was a knock at his door, he successfully hid from the Germans, but his brother Bernard was found and forced to work in a labor camp. Having heard many such stories about this terrible war, Wendy is grateful to be able to raise her children in a peaceful country.